# THE EARS OF LOUIS

# THE EARS OF LOUIS

## CONSTANCE C. GREENE
### Illustrated by Nola Langner

A Yearling Book

TO REBECCA, MAURA, AND JUDITH SULLIVAN

Published by
Dell Publishing Co., Inc.
1 Dag Hammarskjold Plaza
New York, New York 10017

Yearling ® TM 913705, Dell Publishing Co., Inc.

ISBN: 0-440-42269-8

This edition published by arrangement with The Viking Press, Inc.
Printed in the United States of America
First Yearling printing—October 1977

CW

Louis had been doing fine in life until he hit first grade. He could crack his knuckles really loud, he could skip a stone over the water so it bounced five, sometimes six, times.

He also wasn't bad at mumblety peg.

That was four years ago.

Then cousin Marge came calling from Cincinnati. She and Louis' mother were drinking tea in the living room when he got home from school.

"My, my," cousin Marge said, peering sharply at him, "haven't seen you since you were a pup. You've grown some but not as much as I would've thought."

"I was never a pup," Louis said.

"Where *do* you suppose he got such big ears?"

cousin Marge said, as if he hadn't spoken. "Certainly not from *my* side of the family."

"Louis' ears aren't big," his mother said in a stiff voice. "Besides, remember Clark Gable."

"Who's Clark Gable?" Louis asked.

"He was a famous movie star and very handsome," his mother said. "He always got the girl."

The last thing in the world Louis wanted was to get the girl. Still, a famous movie star.

Next, Louis could remember sliding down the slide at school. He closed his eyes against the rush of air and the ground crowding up at him. It was like flying.

"Hey, Elephant Boy," a voice said, "you'd better watch it. The wind gets tangled up in those ears, you might wind up in Alaska."

Louis had opened his eyes to a ring of mouths, all opened wide, laughing. He had put his hands over his ears to shut out the sound, or maybe to hide them. He wasn't sure. All he knew was they were laughing at him.

Louis thought that if he kept quiet and pretended he didn't mind, they'd stop and life would be as it had been before.

What made it worse was you'd never notice his

mother and father's ears, his brother Tom's were teeny and his baby sister's you could hardly see, they were so small. It was a wonder she heard anything at all.

Some days were worse than others. On a bad day, Louis went home and kicked his bed until his toe throbbed. Then he hid the blanket Tom couldn't go to sleep without and once, he even punched his baby sister in the stomach. Her stomach was so fat she hardly felt a thing. She blew spit bubbles at him which made him madder than before.

Louis started taping his ears to the side of his head with Scotch tape. He'd wait until Tom fell asleep in the next bed. He didn't want Tom to know. When he'd finished taping, he'd kneel down beside his bed and pray to God to make his ears small and his muscles big. In the morning, his ears were still big and his muscles small.

It was a bad combination.

Skinny Ernie was the worst. He'd lie in wait behind a tree, then pop out, shouting, "You're some sweet kid, Sugar Bowl!"

Louis would crack his knuckles, yell "Race you!" and run like the wind. Away from one tormentor and into the path of another.

"Dumbo, Dumbo, how's about a sack of peanuts for lunch?" someone else would taunt.

That was why Louis needed big muscles. To knock their blocks off.

After times like these, Louis always had the same dream. In it, he was winning a race. He was passing everybody, he was way out ahead. He was first crossing the finish line. Before he could stop himself, he took off into the air, the wind caught in his ears, and he dipped high and low, like a kite, on his way to Alaska.

Down below, they were laughing again. The sound billowed up at him and his face was hot with shame. When he woke, his mother was standing by his bed.

"What's the matter, Louis? You were shouting in your sleep. Are you all right?" she asked anxiously.

"I'm O.K.," Louis mumbled, so she'd go away and leave him alone. "I'm fine."

Louis' friend Matthew lived far out in the country in a house so old the floors sloped. When Louis went to visit, he and Matthew put out their arms to balance themselves as they ran through the dining room into the downstairs bedroom. The windows were made of many panes of glass which had bubbles in them and there were wooden shutters which locked on the inside. Matthew said they were Indian shutters. Settlers locked them when the Indians attacked. Sometimes Louis and Matthew crouched down low in front of the windows, peering out into the night, imagining they saw a man carrying a tomahawk behind every tree. The sound of the television in the kitchen was very reassuring.

The fireplaces in Matthew's house were so large both Louis and Matthew and Jenny, Matthew's sister, could all stand upright inside. Matthew's room was on the third floor. It had only one window but that window looked out at an apple tree. That made up for a lot of things. Matthew had pried up a piece of one of the wide floor boards. Underneath was a space about six inches long and six inches wide. Just the right size to hide things in. It held some dried worms from last year, a box of marbles, a set of false teeth, three old eyeglass frames without glass and a number of other treasures.

Louis and Matthew talked very little. Matthew's father called them "the silent wonders." They sat on the bank of the river that flowed through Matthew's back yard for hours, staring into the water, counting stones on the river bottom. Or shading their eyes, like Daniel Boone, looking out into the woods for deer or a rattlesnake. Once in a while, they'd drop a string with a worm attached into the water, hoping for a fish to bite.

Once, Matthew told Louis, he'd found a heron with a broken wing standing in the river. He and his father had thrown an old sheet over the heron's head to keep him from panicking, and had taken him to the Humane Society.

"What happened to him?" Louis wanted to know.

"Probably when the wing got better, they let him go," Matthew said. Louis hoped so. Matthew was an authority on wild life. He read books about bears and turtles and beavers. Bears sleep six months at a stretch and deer shed their antlers and grow a whole new pair, he told Louis.

Every day after school Matthew set his Havaheart traps. He had two, one very small to catch rats, weasels, and chipmunks. The other, a birthday present, was bigger.

"With that one," Matthew said, "I might get a muskrat or a skunk." Louis and Matthew often watched a muskrat family, father and mother leading the way, swim along the river bank sedately, in single file, the babies in a neat row, until they came to their home, a hole burrowed into the river bank. Louis thought watching that muskrat family was one of the best things he had ever done.

Matthew never called anybody names. He took people for what they were. He never got wild and crazy, like some kids, running and shrieking and hitting people on the head. But the best thing about him was the way he looked. He had the roundest face Louis had ever seen. Matthew looked, Louis thought, like the man in the moon. Or like pictures he'd seen of the man in the moon in old storybooks. Before the astronauts got up there and found out there weren't any living creatures on the moon. Louis was sorry to hear that. But maybe there were men who'd got word the astronauts were on their way so they hid in a crater or something. Matthew agreed with him that this was a possibility.

Matthew was round all over. He had round pink cheeks and round gray eyes and a round stomach. Even his nose holes were round. If Louis could've looked like anyone he wanted, he would've chosen to look like Matthew.

Last time he'd gone to play at Matthew's, Louis had worn his football helmet. He'd decided to wear it all the time to hide his ears. Anyway, it was football season so he had a good excuse.

They got some cookies and milk and took them to the river bank. Louis kept his helmet on while he ate.

"Why do you keep that thing on all the time?" Matthew asked.

"Because I'm sick and tired of being called Dumbo and Elephant Ears and all that junk," Louis said.

Matthew looked at the water.

"Don't pay any attention to them," he finally said. "I think your ears are nice."

"Why?" Louis said.

"Well," said Matthew, "when the sun shines through them, they're all pink and everything."

"Oh," said Louis.

One day right after school started, Louis' mother bought him three new turtleneck shirts. He wore the yellow one first. At lunch time, he hooked his new shirt over his ears and tucked it under his chin while he ate his egg salad sandwich.

"What a slob!" skinny Ernie said. He unwrapped his marshmallow fluff sandwich. "Where'd you get such a pair of handles?" Ernie said, his mouth full of marshmallow fluff.

Talk about slobs. If the bell hadn't rung just then, Louis might've pushed the second half of Ernie's sandwich in his face.

Louis had orders to wait for Tom to walk him home. Tom was six and afraid of lots of things. Big dogs, roller coasters, and thunder and lightning among them.

Louis walked so fast that day Tom had a tough time keeping up. When they got home, Louis' mother asked him if he'd go next door to Mrs. Beeble's to borrow an onion.

There was nothing in the world Louis liked better than to be sent on an errand to Mrs. Beeble's. Except for visiting Matthew. But he had had a hard day and he felt like giving his mother guff.

"I don't like onions," he said.

"We're having stew and you can't have stew without an onion," his mother said. She smiled at him. "You look beautiful in your new shirt, Louis. But you'd look even more beautiful if you didn't have egg salad all over your front. Why don't you go and change into another shirt?"

"Oh, Mom," Louis turned the corners of his mouth down and frowned. He pretended he didn't like it when his mother said he looked beautiful. Mothers thought their kids were beautiful even if they were as ugly as sin. Still, he couldn't help smiling. He took the stairs three at a time and put on his new blue turtleneck and his football helmet and went next door to see Mrs. Beeble.

Mrs. Beeble had taught Louis how to play poker. They used pink and white candy mints for poker chips. Whoever won got to eat all the chips. Mrs. Beeble had a terrible sweet tooth. Even sweeter than Louis', which was going some. Also, she was a superior poker player.

"You'll have to get up pretty early in the morning to beat Bertha Beeble at poker," she'd told him when they first started to play.

That had been two years ago when Louis was only eight. He'd taken her at her word and set his alarm clock. The sun wasn't even up when the clock went off and Louis hopped out of bed to check Mrs. Beeble's house. The windows were dark. He'd been up pretty early in the morning but Mrs. Beeble still won.

The best thing about playing poker, Louis thought, was arranging the cards. He liked fixing his in a little fan shape. He especially liked getting all one color. All hearts was best of all.

The door opened even before he knocked. Mrs. Beeble was nearsighted without her glasses, which she always misplaced. She squinted at him.

"It's Louis, is it?" she said. "Your head is so big in that contraption I didn't know you. Come on in and take that thing off. All that pressure, it's enough to addle the brains."

They sat down at the kitchen table. Louis kept his helmet on.

"You got time for a hand or two?" Mrs. Beeble asked, shuffling the cards in a professional way that Louis would never master.

He nodded and Mrs. Beeble dealt with the speed of light. She arranged her cards the same way. Louis took much longer, especially when the cards were new and slippery, as they were today.

"I have very few extravagances," Mrs. Beeble had told Louis on numerous occasions, "except that I cannot stand old, limp playing cards. I treat myself to a new pack any time I feel like. I don't crave a mink coat or a diamond ring. My little luxury is a new deck when I want."

Louis dropped his cards twice before he got them organized. He was sorry to see he had only two hearts, and all the rest were black. Mrs. Beeble wore the crafty expression that meant she had a good hand.

"I bet two pinks," she said.

"How about three whites?" Louis put the mints in the center of the table.

"I'll raise you one pink," Mrs. Beeble said, leaning in his direction.

Louis hid his cards against his chest. You had to watch Mrs. Beeble. She had a tendency to cheat. She was very competitive, she had told Louis. Which meant she liked to win even more than he did. Carefully, Louis took a look at his hand.

"I'll raise you one," he said, guarding his cards.

"You don't have to play 'em so close to the vest," Mrs. Beeble said in a huff. "I wasn't looking."

Mrs. Beeble won that hand and the next. She gobbled up all the pink mints. She would.

"Is there any particular reason you keep that thing on inside the house?" Mrs. Beeble asked.

Louis gathered up his hand. He could see a whole mess of red cards even before he got them in order. That was a good sign.

"It's my ears," he said when he'd finally got things set to his liking. "I'm sick and tired of being called names. They tease me." Louis started to shout. "Ernie calls me Dumbo and lots of other things. So I'm wearing my football helmet so they can't see my ears." He felt like throwing his cards against the wall but something told him Mrs. Beeble wouldn't approve.

"You're among friends," she said. "Your ears look all right to me. I subscribe to the theory that a man with good-sized ears is a man with character. It's like being bald. Give me a bald man with good-sized ears any day in the week. I bet two pinks," Mrs. Beeble said.

Louis had to think for a minute. He didn't like to talk and play poker at the same time. It was confusing.

"Besides," Mrs. Beeble said, "you ever hear of Clark Gable?"

"Yeah," Louis said glumly, "he always got the girl."

"Nothing wrong with that, is there? What's your bet?" She leaned towards him.

"I bet three whites," Louis said.

He won that hand and the next one.

"Time to quit," Mrs. Beeble said briskly. "Got to start my supper." Louis had noticed she often had to start her supper or do some crocheting or make a telephone call just as he started to win.

"I'll tell you one thing, though, and that's that that helmet won't get rid of the problem," she said, filling a huge pot with water. "They'll still be there when you take it off. I'll put on my thinking cap and come up with something better."

"What're you having for supper?" Louis asked.

"Spaghetti. With my super duper Bertha Beeble sauce," she said. Mrs. Beeble had spaghetti about

five nights a week. The other times she ate a soft-boiled egg and a dish of cottage cheese.

"I fight the battle of the flesh constantly," she told Louis. "I can't afford to let down my defenses for one second."

"I almost forgot," Louis said. "My mother says can she please borrow an onion?"

Mrs. Beeble burrowed around in a tired-looking paper sack and came up with an onion with a long, pointy tail growing out of one end.

"This one is a little long in the tooth," she said, "but it'll have to do."

Louis said goodbye and started home. He wondered if Mrs. Beeble minded eating supper alone every night. He didn't think he'd like it. Except then he could chew with his mouth open, put his elbows on the table, and burp as much as he wanted. Maybe eating alone was fun. Once in a while.

Onions with teeth? He'd have to think about it a while to get used to the idea.

It was the end of September when Miss Carmichael told her fifth grade they could take their names off the fronts of their desks.

"I've got you all committed to memory," she said. "I know who you all are now."

Louis tore his name paper into tiny shreds and stuffed them into his lunch bag. That was a relief. He felt safer, more himself, without his name written on yellow paper in big black letters for the whole world to see.

Calvin Leffert, who was the biggest kid in the whole school, almost as big as a small man, wiped his nose on his sleeve and said in a loud voice, "She doesn't know who *I* am. Nobody knows who I am. My mother nor my father nor nobody."

"Calvin, that's enough," Miss Carmichael said. She was always telling Calvin that. For once, Louis had to agree with Calvin. Nobody knew who he, Louis, was, either.

Miss Carmichael clasped her hands in front of her purple dress. Her fingernails matched her dress. So did her lipstick. Miss Carmichael was nobody's fool, Louis thought.

"I'd like each of you to write a story or a poem or draw a picture," she said. "We're going to have a school newspaper and we'd like each and every one of you to participate. Mr. Anderson will choose the best entries from each grade and they'll be published in the first issue."

Mr. Anderson was the principal. He had big flat feet and a tiny mustache and looked like Adolf Hitler. The first day of school Louis had raised his arm and said "Achtung" under his breath to Mr. Anderson. He didn't know what made him do it. He couldn't stop himself. Fortunately, Mr. Anderson only frowned and said, "Move along, please."

The kids groaned and said "What a gross out" to Miss Carmichael's suggestion. Amy Adams, who sat in front of Louis, waved a bunch of papers in the air.

"These are poems I wrote," Amy said. She reminded Louis of cousin Marge. There was something about the way she pursed her mouth and smiled. Louis concentrated on hypnotizing Amy. He pointed both hands with the fingers stuck straight out at Amy's back. "Sleep, sleep," he said in a sing-song voice under his breath. Amy went right on talking about how she had a lot more poems at home she could bring in.

Louis ate lunch with Matthew and another boy named John. Sometimes they traded sandwiches. Today John had a cucumber sandwich with mayonnaise and Matthew had cream cheese and walnuts so Louis stuck with his egg salad. Louis thought anybody who ate cucumber with mayonnaise or cream cheese and walnuts was crazy.

"I caught a chipmunk in my Havaheart trap last night," Matthew said. "I used an old doughnut for bait."

"I didn't know chipmunks liked old doughnuts," Louis said, chewing on a piece of celery.

"They don't," Matthew said.

"My mother made me pick sticks up off the lawn after school," John said. His mother was always making him pick up his room or his books or sticks off the lawn. Louis didn't like to go to John's house much. His mother made him take off his shoes before he came inside.

"Tell your little friend to take off his shoes, too," John's mother said when Louis came to the door. She stood and watched while Louis took off his shoes. His sock had a big hole in the toe. John's mother shook her head and said "tsk-tsk" the way people did in the funny papers. Louis had never heard anyone say "tsk-tsk" out loud before. It didn't make him like John's mother any better.

From then on, whenever John asked Louis over to play, Louis said, "Come to my house instead." John usually did.

Louis looked in his lunch bag. It was empty except for some celery leaves and the pieces of his name paper. He threw it in the trash can.

"I'm going to see if I can get a game with the big guys," he said, putting on his helmet.

"They won't let you play," Matthew said. "Not those guys. They're tough customers. You might get your head beat in."

The same thought had occurred to Louis but he went out to the playground anyway. The sixth graders played there every day at recess.

Louis sat on the sidelines, watching and waiting.

"Forty-two, sixty-three, hike," they hollered, milling around, not doing much of anything. Louis got down on one knee and rested both fists on the

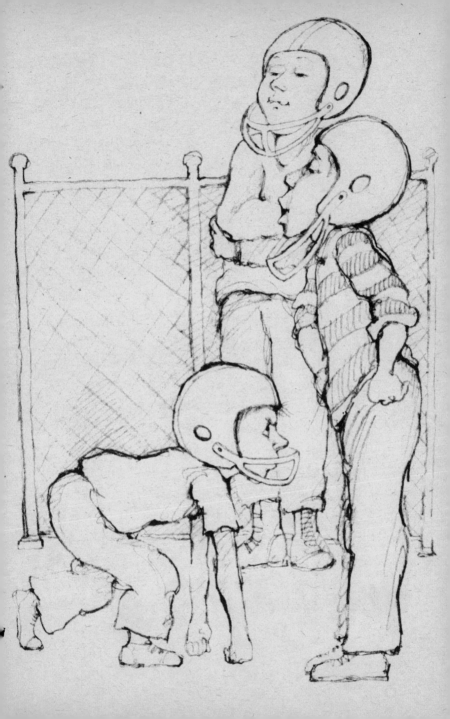

ground, the way he'd seen the pros do in newspaper pictures. It was a very tiring position, he discovered. No one paid any attention to him but no one called him names, either.

Louis hoped someone would get hurt or something. Then he could come in as a substitute. When the bell rang, no one had a sprained ankle or even a cut on the cheek. It was discouraging.

Miss Carmichael sent him to the washroom to clean up. He walked past Mr. Anderson's office and saw Mr. Anderson talking on the telephone, smiling at his fingernails. It was the first time Louis had seen him smile. He wondered if whoever was on the other end of the phone was telling a joke.

Louis peeked through the window of the first grade and saw Tom leaning on his elbow, sucking his thumb. He couldn't tell whether Tom was awake or asleep. Louis washed his hands and face without soap. He scrubbed himself vigorously with a harsh paper towel. He looked at himself in the mirror and filled his cheeks with air so his face was almost as round as Matthew's. Maybe that way, his ears wouldn't seem so big. But his ears looked just as big as before.

On the way back to his room, Louis was stopped by a sixth grader.

"I'm conducting a survey," he said, "and you're just the guy I want to see. As the anchor man on this survey, I'm reporting my findings after a thorough investigation. The gist of it is, do people with big ears hear better than people with small ears?" The big kid took out a pencil and a pad and looked at Louis, waiting.

Louis looked at his shoes. He thought about butting his head into the big kid's stomach and then running away. He decided against it.

"Hey, man on the street, does a kid like you hear more things than a kid with ordinary size ears?" The sixth grader was getting impatient.

Louis cracked his knuckles. The buzzing in his head was so loud the cracking noise sounded faint and far away. He wished he could give the kid a couple of karate chops. Just enough to knock him out, not kill him.

"I've gotta go to the boy's room," Louis said. He turned and walked back to the washroom, put his head under the cold water faucet and turned it on. When his hair was wet and his cheeks cool, he carefully dried himself off. Then he opened the door and looked out. The sixth grader had gone.

"I was about to send out the police," Miss Carmichael said. She and Louis looked at each other.

"We're on our blue book, page ten," Miss Carmichael said, and turned to the blackboard. "Please pay attention."

Maybe Miss Carmichael *did* know who he was, after all.

The next day Louis had just got home from school, thrown his books on the table and was leaning into the refrigerator to see what was good to eat when the telephone rang.

"Bertha Beeble here," a voice said. "May I speak to Louis, please?"

Louis was delighted. He never got telephone calls, except for Matthew telling him what he'd caught in his Havaheart trap.

"Louis here," he said in a squeaky voice.

"I've got a present for you," Mrs. Beeble said. "I think you might like it. When you get a chance, come on over."

Louis was halfway across the lawn before he remembered he'd forgotten to shut the refrigerator door. He raced back, slammed it closed, then raced again to Mrs. Beeble's. By the time he got there, he was so out of breath he couldn't speak.

"Step into the parlor," Mrs. Beeble said. Only once before, on New Year's Day, Louis had been invited to step into Mrs. Beeble's parlor and that was to drink eggnog.

"I got it in an antique shop," Mrs. Beeble said, handing him a small box. "Open it, quick."

"Gee," Louis said, staring at the lumpy piece of gray metal lying on a somewhat dingy wad of cotton. He didn't know what else to say so he said "Gee" again. "Thanks."

"Aha!" Mrs. Beeble snatched up the present and swung it back and forth. "You don't know what it is, do you? It's an amulet, a talisman with a face engraved upon it. Look," she said, taking it over to the window, "see?" Louis could make out a man's head wearing a crown and a pair of ears that stuck out on either side of his long, narrow head.

"In view of our conversation the other day," Mrs. Beeble said, "I know you won't take umbrage when I say the minute I saw it, it reminded me of you."

She tied a long piece of string through the loop at

the top of the talisman and slipped it over Louis'
head.

"This is a good luck charm," Mrs. Beeble said. "It
will have a powerful influence on you."

"It will?" Louis looked down at his amulet, which
hung almost to his bellybutton.

"We'll have to take a reef in that sail," Mrs. Beeble
said firmly. She cut a piece off the string and retied
it around his neck.

Louis got a lump in his throat, just thinking about
what they'd say when they saw him wearing a
necklace.

"Tuck it inside your shirt," she told him. "That
way, it's a secret, yours and mine. Don't expect miracles, though. You've got to believe in its powers but
miracles are harder. You have to work for them. This
will ward off evil, if you let it." She shuffled the
cards. "Got time for a hand or two?" she said.

"Sure." Louis followed Mrs. Beeble into the
kitchen. "Do you wear an amulet?" he asked.

"There's been a lot of water over the dam since
the time when a good luck charm would do me any
good," she said. "No sense crying over spilt milk, I
always say. But when I was young, you wouldn't
catch me without one." Rapidly, she dealt the cards.

"Oh, ho ho," she chortled as she picked up her hand. "You got that lucky charm just in time. You're going to need it today."

Mrs. Beeble won the first hand, then Louis won three in a row. He had a big pile of pink and white mints in front of him. She had only four.

"First bet!" Louis cried. It was his turn to deal. He had all hearts.

"From now on," Mrs. Beeble said glumly after Louis had won still another hand, "you're going to have to take that off and put it on the table. That way, you don't have the advantage."

Absent-mindedly, Mrs. Beeble popped two pink mints in her mouth.

Louis tapped her on the arm.

"I won that last hand," he said.

"You don't have to get sore about it," Mrs. Beeble said. "Anyway, it's. . . ."

"Yeah, I know. Time for supper."

"How'd you know?" Mrs. Beeble asked.

Louis was almost home before he remembered his manners. He ran back to thank Mrs. Beeble again for his amulet. She was sitting at the kitchen table playing solitaire. Her face was old and sad and looked different from the way it looked when she and

Louis played poker. He thought of knocking on the door and calling out. Then he changed his mind. Somehow, he didn't think she'd want anyone looking at her when she was like that. He tiptoed down the steps and went home.

The light was on in the kitchen so Louis pressed his nose against the window and peered in, pretending he was a lonely traveler crossing the moors, looking for a place to lay his head. He saw his mother talking on the telephone and spooning cereal into his baby sister's mouth. Tom was watching TV and sucking his thumb.

Louis howled like a werewolf. No one paid any attention except Wilma, who got up and began pacing back and forth, back and forth. Wilma, Louis' father said, was a dog with a persecution complex. She always thought somebody or something was out to get her. Wilma was very tense and nervous at times. The way she was pacing, Louis knew this was one of those times.

He hung up his hat and jacket and watched TV. Click, click, Tom's thumb said against the roof of his mouth. Tom had a giant callous where his teeth hit his thumb every time he put it in his mouth. The callous was shiny and hard and yellow and seemed almost to have a life of its own. As far as Louis was concerned, that callous was the only good thing about thumb sucking. It would be kind of neat to have a callous like that.

"You want to go out, Wilma?" Louis said. Wilma smelled bad. That meant she'd been in somebody's garbage can. She turned her big brown eyes on Louis, asking for sympathy. Click, click, her toenails beat a tattoo on the floor.

Tom took his thumb out of his mouth.

"I'm going to be a hero when I grow up," he said.

"Har de har har," Louis said, very scornful. "Whoever heard of a hero who sucks his thumb? Some hero you'll make."

"Heroes never die," Tom said.

"John Wayne dies," Louis said.

"No he doesn't." Tom put his thumb back in his mouth.

"I bet he got killed at least four times," Louis said.

Tom shook his head.

Louis thought hard. He couldn't remember when John Wayne got killed. His mind was like a big flat stretch of desert with no footprints on it.

The cartoon ended and a commercial came on about a lady who called up her friend from the drug store because she didn't know what to do about occasional irregularity.

"Try prunes!" Louis shouted, and began to feel better.

You smell like Wilma when she gets in the neighbors' garbage cans," Louis told Matthew next day.

"I caught a skunk in my Havaheart trap," Matthew said, "and when I let him out, he sprayed me. He was scared." Matthew made excuses for the skunk. "My mother gave me a bath in tomato juice. It's supposed to kill the smell but I guess it didn't do a very good job." Matthew was pink around the edges. His hair was pink too.

"She didn't want me home today. She said of all days I had to get sprayed by a skunk. She's having her bridge club over so she poured a giant can of tomato juice over me and sent me to school."

Calvin Leffert stood up and said in a loud voice,

"I smell skunk." Maybe Calvin wasn't too smart but there wasn't anything wrong with his nose.

"Sit down, Calvin," Miss Carmichael said. She opened the door to the supply closet and looked around. Then she went to the coat room and peered inside a few jackets and an old sneaker somebody had left a long time ago.

"Whoever is responsible for that odor please come forward," Miss Carmichael said.

Louis drew a picture of a giant genie coming out of a tiny bottle. Amy Adams minced up to Miss Carmichael's desk. "I brought in some more of my poems for the newspaper," Amy said.

Louis wondered what would happen if, all of a sudden, he punched Amy in the nose.

"I know skunk when I smell skunk," Calvin said even louder. "Some smart aleck caught it good."

"If any one of you is hiding an animal in here, I shall have to send that person to Mr. Anderson's office. He will deal with the matter."

"It's me, Miss Carmichael," Matthew said, standing up, looking round and pink and sad. "I got sprayed by a skunk before I came to school when I let him out of my Havaheart trap and my mother poured a can of tomato juice over me but it didn't do any good."

Amy put her hand over her mouth and giggled.

Calvin pounded his fist on his forehead. "I knew it," he shouted. "I knew it."

Mr. Anderson came into the room unannounced.

"Well, now," he said, smiling and stroking his mustache, "how is the fifth grade getting on today?"

"Oh dear," Miss Carmichael said, putting a handkerchief over her nose. "We seem to be having a little problem. One of our students was sprayed by a skunk and there is a rather strong odor. . ."

Mr. Anderson backed slowly out the door. "I do detect something," he said. "Pardon me. . . ." And he disappeared as suddenly as he'd come.

"I'll call your mother, Matthew, and ask her to come get you," Miss Carmichael said.

"She's having her bridge club and she's making sandwiches and my father took the car to the station so she can't come get me," Matthew said.

"Well then," Miss Carmichael gave an exasperated sigh, "I'll give you some work to take out in the hall. You can sit on the bench and do it there."

When the lunch bell rang, Louis and John and Matthew sat together in a corner of the lunchroom. "I don't care how bad you smell," Louis said.

John didn't say anything. He held his nose with his left hand and ate his sandwich with his right.

"I'm glad I have two friends anyway," Matthew said dolefully. "How's about trading half a peanut butter and bacon for half whatever you've got?"

"Hey kid," the sixth grader conducting the survey said to Louis, "you ready with an answer for me yet? Do you hear better with those huge ears than these two creeps," he pointed at Matthew and John, "with their tiny ones?"

Under his red turtleneck, Louis felt the weight of his amulet and saw the bulge it made in the middle of his chest. He hadn't told anyone at school, not even Matthew and John, about Mrs. Beeble's present.

Get to work, Louis said to his charm. Ward off this evil.

"This is a very important survey I'm conducting. I don't want to have to get tough," the kid said. "Cough up an answer."

Louis held his lunch bag to his mouth and coughed elaborately into it. Then he handed the bag to the boy and said, "Look inside and you'll find it."

"Wise guy," the kid said disgustedly. He threw the empty bag onto the floor and walked away.

"Nice work," John said, still holding his nose. He sounded as if he had a terrible cold. "I'm proud of you, Louis. A big guy like that might've let you have it right between the eyes. What's he mean anyway? Your ears aren't huge, they're only big. I remember when you first were my friend in second grade, in Miss Johnson's class, I thought you had giant-sized ears but then, after a while I didn't even think about your ears at all."

Louis smiled. He liked that.

The three of them sat chewing thoughtfully.

"I think what I'll do next time," Matthew said, peering between the slices of bread to make sure he wasn't eating anything he didn't like, "is, I'll only use old doughnuts for bait."

"What'd you use to catch the skunk?" Louis asked.

"Fish heads. I went to the fish market and the guy was just putting out the garbage and I found a whole mess of fish heads. Skunks love fish heads."

"How'd you know that?" Louis asked.

"My grandmother, she has about ten cats and she told me skunks were always jumping into her garbage and dragging out the empty cat food cans," Matthew said. "It figures if they like cat food, they'd like fish heads, right?"

John nodded vigorously.

Louis said, "Cat food's expensive and fish heads are free. I bet you thought of that too."

Matthew smiled. "I'm thinking every minute," he said.

"No wonder you smell like Wilma," Louis said. He put on his football helmet and jogged out to the playground. A game was already in progress. Louis ran back and forth on the sidelines.

"Hey, pass it here. Let's have that ball. Toss it to me," they shouted. Once somebody made a touchdown. The cheers were deafening. Louis shouted as hard as anyone on the team. He tried to imagine what it would be like to have all those people cheering for him.

"Yeah, Louis. Yeah, Louis," they would shout. They'd clap him on the back, arms would go around his shoulders, and they'd hoist him up in the air and carry him off the field in triumph.

"Hey there, Elephant Ears!" The familiar words brought Louis back to the world he lived in. "How come you're not out in Disneyland? They sure could use you out there, I bet." It was a friend of Ernie's, a boy with little eyes set close to his nose.

This time Louis couldn't think of a single comeback. When the bell rang, he loped back into his room, pretending he hadn't heard.

On Saturday Louis helped his father rake leaves for a while. Not for very long. He'd rake a huge pile, then jump smack in the middle and lie still, looking at the sky, thinking about things.

"Listen, Louis," his father finally said. "I appreciate your efforts on my behalf but in the long run I think I can finish up faster by myself."

Louis hopped up and said "O.K., Dad." He'd seen a sign for a garage sale yesterday on his way home from school. There was nothing Louis liked better than a garage sale. They were right up his alley. They were full of things like old bicycles, old ice skates, a table that might be perfect for keeping his rock collection on or an old book with "To Ezra, with love from Grandmother, Christmas, 1906" written in it in a fine, spidery handwriting. Probably Ezra would much rather have had a train or a stuffed snake or something really good. But Louis had noticed grandmothers liked to give kids books. They thought books improved kids' minds. Louis wasn't absolutely sure this was always true.

He followed the signs until he came to a house badly in need of paint. There were several card tables set up in the front yard. Louis looked around but he couldn't see any garage.

"Hey there, sonny," said an old man guarding the merchandise.

"How come you call it a garage sale when there's no garage?" Louis asked.

The old man said, "What's the use of having a garage when we don't have any car?"

Louis didn't have any answer to that.

"You're just in time for bargains," the old man said, winking. "Business isn't all that good. Just had a lady with the biggest shopping bag this side of Texas. You got to watch them with the shopping bags. In the flick of an eye they can load up and make off without paying a cent if you don't keep a close eye out."

Louis was glad he didn't have a shopping bag with

him. A plastic owl (25¢), a set of chipped mugs that said World's Fair, 1939 (50¢), and an old pipe (30¢) were all desirable items. Louis had learned to take his time choosing. It didn't pay to rush into buying anything. A couple of spotted ties (25¢ each) might do for Christmas presents for his father.

The old man looked carefully over his shoulder toward the house. "You can have your pick of the lot for less than they're marked," he whispered, although there was no one but him and Louis to hear. "She just went inside to catch one of those giveaway shows on TV. She doesn't like to miss one."

A window in the house opened and a fat lady leaned out.

"Don't you go giving things away now, Poppa," she called. "We're out to make some money, not to play Santa Claus."

"Yes, Agnes," the old man shouted. He busied himself with rearranging items. When the window slammed down, he said to Louis, "That Agnes, she's a tiger. She sleeps with her eyes open."

Louis imagined the fat woman stretched out on a bed, hands clasped on her chest, staring up at the ceiling all night long. She must be awful tired when it was time to get up.

"Try hefting these," the old man said, pointing

to a set of junior bar bells lying on the ground. "Guaranteed to make you the strongest kid on the block."

Louis tried to pick up the bar bells. He got them as far as his knees. They were heavy, junior or not.

"A little effort every day and first thing you know you'll have them up in the air," the old man gave encouragement.

"How much are they?" Louis asked.

"How much you got?" he said.

"My allowance," Louis said. If he bought the bar bells, he wouldn't have enough for a roll of Scotch tape. On the other hand, if his muscles got bigger, he could knock their blocks off and he wouldn't need the Scotch tape. He took the quarter out of his pocket.

"Agnes will have a conniption when she finds out I let 'em go that cheap," the old man said, pocketing the quarter. "They're yours."

Louis tried lifting them again. No luck.

"How am I going to get them home?" he said.

"Good thought. Good thought. You got your head on all right, sonny." The old man pondered. "I could let you have the loan of that." He pointed to a battered red wagon. Louis had its twin at home. "If you promise to bring it back."

Louis promised and together he and the old man loaded the bar bells into the wagon.

"Wooo-eee," the old man said when they'd finished. "Time was when I could've tossed those things in the air like they was made of spun sugar. I'm out of shape. In my prime, Charles Atlas had to watch out."

"Who's Charles Atlas?" Louis asked.

"Only the strongest man in the world," the old man said. "He had muscles like iron bands, like it says in the poem. Nobody messed around with old Charlie. Not if they was smart, they didn't."

When Louis got home with his prize, he pulled the wagon right up to the kitchen door. He eased it through and into the dining room, then to the foot of the stairs.

"What's that?" his father asked.

"I bought it at a garage sale for a quarter," Louis said. "It's to make your muscles big like Charles Atlas and then you can punch people who make fun of you."

Instead of saying "You shouldn't spend your money on junk," the way he usually did after one of Louis' purchases, his father examined the bar bells.

"I can get them up to my knees," Louis said. "But if I practice I'll get better every day."

"I wouldn't be surprised," his father said. He carried them upstairs and put them on the floor by Louis' bed. When he'd left, Louis untied his amulet and took it over to the window to examine it more carefully.

The face was very long and thin, the ears very large. Larger even than mine, Louis thought. The crown on the head made them look worse. Louis wondered how he'd look wearing a crown. Like some kind of a nut, he decided. He ran his fingers over the amulet. Things had been no better or no worse since Mrs. Beeble had given it to him. On the other hand, he had the bar bells. He might be on his way to becoming another Charles Atlas.

If that was so, skinny Ernie and others had better watch their step. Louis took his cigar box out from under the mattress. He planned to choose something from it to give to Mrs. Beeble in return for her present to him.

The plastic bag full of bird feathers was one of his favorites but somehow he didn't think Mrs. Beeble would like it. He had a really good collection of foreign coins his grandparents added to from time to time. But what good would they be to Mrs. Beeble if she never left the country?

Maybe a paperback book would be a good idea.

Every time the school librarian threw out the beat-up ones, Louis retrieved them from the waste basket and brought them home. He was thinking of having a garage sale of his own one of these days.

There was nothing in the cigar box that was right for Mrs. Beeble. He'd have to keep looking for just the right thing.

He got his stack of mail order catalogues left over from last Christmas out from under his bed. Everything was too expensive. Maybe when he returned the wagon to the old man he'd find something at the garage sale that he'd missed today.

Louis took the wagon back after lunch on Sunday. The old man and Agnes hadn't bothered to take the signs down and it had rained during the night. The pieces of cardboard they'd used were shriveled up so the letters were blurred and hard to read.

"Hey there, sonny." The old man stood in the same spot. The card tables seemed to hold the same items. The plastic owl, World's Fair mugs, and pipe were still there. Only the spotted ties were gone.

"Those ties had a bit of life in 'em," the old man said, opening his sweater to show Louis. He wore the red and blue one. "I knew I could trust you. Agnes, now, she hears all this stuff about kids nowadays. She figured we could kiss that wagon goodbye.

I knew you'd be back. What can I do for you today?"

"I'm looking for a present for Mrs. Beeble," Louis said. "She gave me this," and, to his own surprise, he pulled out his amulet.

"Handsome, a beautiful piece of work," the old man said.

A window in the house opened and the fat lady called, "Poppa! You know what I told you. You stop giving things away. I'm going down for a nap now, Poppa. Didn't hardly close my eyes all last night." The window closed sharply.

"Didn't I tell you she sleeps with her eyes open?" the old man said. "Not many left like Agnes."

Louis thought that was probably a very good thing.

"How'd you do with the bar bells?" He felt Louis' muscle. "Keep after it, sonny. Perseverance pays off." He put his hand in his pocket and came up with a collection of things Matthew would've liked for his hiding place. A ring with a blue stone, three dice, a key ring and four pennies.

"I spent all my money yesterday," Louis said.

"The story of my life." The old man sighed. "I'm going to let you in on a secret. This here is not a genuine sapphire. On account of that, I can let you have it for nothing." He handed the ring to Louis, who wondered what Agnes would say. If she ever found out.

"I could pay you next week when I get my allowance," Louis offered.

"Don't mention it. I like giving things to deserving people. When the present fits the person, like those bar bells, it makes me feel good." The old man shook hands with Louis. "I hope Mrs. Beeble and that ring are compatible. Stop by some time and let me know."

"O.K.," Louis said. "Thanks a lot." He started out with a springy step. He felt good.

"Hey Elephant Ears, we know you! Come out from under your disguise!" The voices rang in Louis' head. He didn't know who was calling him. He didn't stop to find out. Instead, he walked faster, faster until he had a pain in his side and his heart was pounding. Whoever it was didn't catch up. Louis made up his mind. He'd keep working at those bar bells and his muscles, combined with his good luck charm, would make him invincible. Then when Ernie and the boy with the little eyes called him names, he'd turn around and punch them in the face. Wham! Pow!

Louis rang Mrs. Beeble's door bell and when she

answered, he handed her the ring. "It's for you," he said. "I was digging in my back yard for worms and I found a chest full of treasure. Probably pirates buried it there a long time ago."

Mrs. Beeble didn't flick an eye. "It's lovely," she said. "You were nice to think of me. I'll cherish it always."

Louis didn't know why he got carried away and told stories like that. It didn't happen often but when it did, he really told a big one. A tall tale, his father called it. Then he usually had to go and spoil it by telling the truth.

"I found a garage sale down the street," he said, "and the old man who was running it gave it to me. For free. That's because I spent my allowance on a pair of bar bells yesterday and I didn't have anything left."

"Of the two stories," Mrs. Beeble said, turning the ring to catch the light, "I prefer the first. At any event, I'm glad you thought of me. I'd ask you in for a hand or two but I'm expecting company." She wore a big white apron and had a sort of plastic cap on her head.

"I'm making steak and kidney pie. My niece and her husband are coming. I'd never think of making steak and kidney pie for myself. It's not much fun to cook just for one person," Mrs. Beeble said. She looked gay and happy. Her cheeks were pink and her eyes sparkled.

Louis backed off from the idea of steak and kidney pie.

"I'll see you," he said. Mrs. Beeble waved and closed the door.

As Louis cut across the yard, a car pulled up and a lady and man got out. They must be Mrs. Beeble's niece and her husband. They looked kind of dried up and sour, Louis thought. Still, he was glad Mrs. Beeble wouldn't be eating alone.

On Monday the impossible happened.

Louis was stationed on the sidelines, watching the big kids mill around, trying to get a game organized.

"Where's Steve? Where's Eddie?" they called.

"Flu. They've got the flu."

"Oh boy, it's not worth it, to have a game with nobody here. We better wait 'til tomorrow. Maybe they'll be back by then."

"Why can't we play with subs?" the boy who seemed to be captain of the team asked. "That's what the pros do. They have subs so if somebody gets hurt, like he racks up his knee or something, the game doesn't get put off, it goes on."

The sixth graders stood with their hands on their

hips and looked over the horizon for subs. Louis resumed his position on one knee with both fists supporting him. He hoped they'd notice him before he got tired.

"How about that little guy? Hey, kid, want to get in the game?"

Considering he'd been waiting and dreaming and hoping for just this minute ever since school started, Louis did a pretty good job of pretending he didn't know who they were talking to.

He got up from the ground and trotted over to the group.

"You mean me?" he said nonchalantly.

"I don't know," the captain said. "He's pretty small. He might get hurt and we'd catch it from Mr. Anderson. He probably wouldn't let us play at all if this little kid got racked up."

Louis put his hands on his hips. "Don't worry about me," he said. "I can take care of myself."

"Listen, we better get going if we're going to play at all. It's almost time for the bell," somebody said.

"Right. Get over there, kid. That's the goal line. If you get hold of the ball, you have to take it over  that line and touch ground with it," the captain explained to Louis.

Louis never touched the ball. He ran back and forth, shouting "Throw it here, over here!" and he got in the huddle. He felt eight feet tall. Just before the bell rang and the game was over for the day, someone kicked a field goal. The ball went slightly astray and got Louis in the stomach.

"You O.K.?" they asked him.

Louis felt a little sick. That kid was no slouch when it came to kicking a field goal, even if his aim wasn't all that hot.

"Sure, I'm fine," he said.

"Time to go, guys. I just heard the bell. You know Mr. Anderson if we're late." They all trotted off the field, Louis following. He really didn't feel so good.

He took off his helmet and made it to the boys' room just in time. It was a good thing his mother had given him a bologna sandwich for lunch and that Matthew was absent that day. Louis hated bologna and so did John, so he'd thrown most of it away.

Louis threw up in the toilet. Usually when he threw up, his mother held his head. He sort of missed her. On the other hand, maybe they wouldn't have let his mother into the boys' room. He stayed until he was sure it was all over, then he went to his classroom.

Miss Carmichael gave him a fishy look.

"Louis," she said, "you've got to learn to come in from whatever it is you do after lunch when you hear the bell. We can't have our students in the fifth grade act as if they're still in the fourth grade. Get to your work now."

Louis didn't trust himself to speak because that would mean opening his mouth and he wasn't absolutely sure that would be a good idea. He sat down and began to copy his arithmetic. Amy Adams turned around and stuck out her tongue at him.

Louis contemplated the back of Amy's neck. He leaned over his desk and opened his mouth just a little. Nothing came out. He was glad and sorry at the same time. If he'd thrown up in class, it would've been embarrassing. On the other hand, if he could've nailed Amy, that would have made his day perfect.

Oh, it was something!" Louis shouted, bursting into the kitchen after school. "I played football with the big kids and I almost made a touchdown and I ran about a million yards and they asked me to play with them again."

"Nononononono," sang Louis' baby sister, sitting in her high chair and shampooing her hair with applesauce.

"Boy, you get away with murder," Louis said to her. "I'd like to see what'd happen to me if I rubbed applesauce in my hair. Probably I couldn't watch TV for a week. Make that two weeks I couldn't watch it."

"Nononononono," she said, rubbing away with great enthusiasm.

"Oh, Lord," Louis' mother said, coming up out of the cellar. She mopped the baby, the walls, and the high chair.

"You should've seen me, Mom," Louis said. "I played football and a kid kicked the ball and it hit me in the stomach so I threw up."

"I thought you looked pale," she said. "Better go up and lie down."

Louis took the jar of silver polish up to his room. He put a big gob on his good luck charm, taking special care with the crown and the ears. He rubbed and polished until it shone. Then he washed it under the faucet.

It was time for a workout with the bar bells. Louis still couldn't get them past his knees but he felt a lot stronger.

"Louis, telephone," his mother called up the stairs.

"Louis here," he said into the receiver, imitating Mrs. Beeble.

"What? What'd you say? Guess what I caught in my Havaheart," Matthew's voice said.

"How come you weren't in school today?"

"I caught another skunk and when I went to let it out, it sprayed me. My mother's boiling. She says she's going to give my traps to the Salvation Army.

I told her if she did, I'd run away. I told her I couldn't go to school. That's what Miss Carmichael said last week. She said if it happened again, I'd better stay home. So my mother made me sit outside in the car while she went to eat lunch with some ladies. I asked her if I could stay home by myself but she said enough was enough and she wanted to keep me where she'd know what I was doing."

"Will you smell all right by tomorrow?" Louis said.

"I better. She bought two quarts of tomato juice and put me in the bathtub and poured it over me and now she's scrubbing out the tub and she's still boiling," Matthew said.

"Guess what?" Louis said. "I played football with the sixth graders today."

"You did?" Matthew said. "How was it? Did anybody tackle you?"

"It was pretty rough," Louis said, "but I did all right. They didn't want to let me play. They said I was too little. But I played anyway and one kid kicked the ball and it hit me in the stomach and I got sick. I almost got sick again, all over Amy Adams."

"Cool," Matthew said. "What stopped you?"

67

"I didn't have anything left in my insides," Louis said. He heard a scream from Matthew's end of the line.

Then silence.

"I have to hang up," Matthew said. "She says I'm dripping all over her new rug."

"O.K.," Louis said. "Stay away from skunks."

Matthew laughed a hollow laugh and hung up.

Tuesday morning Louis woke up feeling very good. Even when he checked his ears and his muscles and they seemed to be too big and too small as they'd always been, he still felt good.

He tucked his amulet inside his shirt, first rubbing it for luck. He didn't go anywhere without that amulet. He found a pair of matching socks in his drawer and he could smell bacon cooking. Everything pointed to a super day.

He wore his helmet to breakfast. From behind his newspaper, his father said, "Take that off while you eat, please." It was amazing what his father could see from behind that paper.

"How'd you know I had it on?" Louis said, taking it off.

"Haven't you?" his father said, still behind his paper.

"Not now," Louis said.

"Come home right after school," his mother said. "I'm taking you for a haircut."

Louis' hair reached the tip of his ears. It was just the right length.

"I don't need a haircut," he said.

Nobody answered.

"Why do I always have to get a haircut just when I like it the way it is?" Louis asked. "How'd you like it if somebody made you get your hair cut every time you thought your hair looked pretty nice? You wouldn't like it at all, that's for sure."

When he got to school, Miss Carmichael told the class she'd only had two people hand in stuff for the newspaper.

"I had hoped for more contributions," she said, looking over the top of her glasses. "A little more co-operation is indicated."

Amy Adams turned around in her seat and smiled graciously. She gave a little wave like the queen of England. Louis put both hands around his own throat and gagged noisily.

At lunch, Louis bolted his sandwich and raced out

to the field. The same guys he'd played with yesterday were already there throwing the ball back and forth talking big. "Hey Charlie, let's have it here. Toss it to me and I'll take it for a hundred yards. Come on, you apes, let's run it down the line," they said.

Louis stood there, smiling, holding his helmet.

"Hi," he said.

Nobody answered. Like this morning at home, it was as if he hadn't spoken. Maybe he'd dreamed up yesterday. But he hadn't dreamed being sick in the boys' room. That much he knew.

Louis put on his helmet and got down in his crouch. The game began, the sun shone on the sixth graders in all their radiance. Louis stood by. The bell rang. It was over.

"Hey, Dumbo, wouldn't they let you play?" Two friends of Ernie's were watching. "They probably figured your ears would get in the way." One of them, the kid with the tiny eyes straddling his nose, advanced upon Louis.

"What's that?" He reached out a grubby hand toward Louis' charm which had worked its way to the outside of his shirt. "Let's see what you got there, old Elephant Ears."

Louis knew if this kid touched his amulet, it would no longer be entirely his. Its power would vanish. He jerked back but the kid was holding on. The string broke and the charm was in the hand of the enemy.

"Give it here," Louis said in a voice that trembled. "Give it here or I'll kill you."

"Go get it." The kid threw the charm as far as he could. Louis followed it with his eyes and ran to the spot where it had fallen. He got down on his hands and knees, searching in the dust. The sun glinted on the newly polished surface and led Louis to it. He picked it up and wiped the dust off with his shirt tail. The face looked up at him, noble and unyielding.

"That's all right," Louis said aloud. "Don't mind those creeps. You're O.K." He cradled it in his hands, checking for damage. There was none. Louis stood up and put the amulet in his pocket. The bell had long since rung. He stood at his classroom door, watching Miss Carmichael write on the blackboard. If he went in now, she'd bawl him out for being late again.

"I'm not up to it," he said to the walls. He went down the hall past Mr. Anderson's office. The principal was on the telephone again, and still smiling. Louis thought Mr. Anderson spent so much time smiling over the telephone he didn't have anything but frowns left when he got off.

Louis wandered around the streets, killing time. He'd have to go back to school to pick up Tom. He wished he could tell time by the sun. He didn't have a watch. When it seemed as if he'd been walking for hours, he went to a candy store and asked the man what time it was.

"Time for you to be in school," the man said, laughing. When he saw the look on Louis' face, he said, "It's two twenty, son."

Louis went back to school. When Tom came out, Louis said "Hurry up" and took giant steps all the way home. "You're going too fast," Tom wailed.

Louis got the ball of string from the drawer in the hall table and ran up the stairs.

"Are you ready to go to the barber?" his mother called.

Louis didn't answer. He measured a piece of string and, using his mother's nail scissors, he cut it off and slipped it through the loop at the top of the amulet.

"Come on, Louis, I'm waiting," his mother said.

He went to the top of the stairs.

"Mom," he said, "would you please tie this for me." He held both ends of the string at the back of his neck and backed up to her.

She didn't ask any questions until she'd got it tied in a double knot. She turned him around so their faces were close together.

"That's very pretty," she said. "What is it?"

"Mrs. Beeble gave it to me," he said. "It's an amulet. A good luck charm. It wards off evil."

"You're awfully young to need to ward off anything," she said. "What do you know of evil?"

"Plenty," Louis said.

She hugged him. "Well, then, I hope you wear your good luck charm until you're an old man." She took the car keys out of her pocket. "Let's go," she said.

"Where?" Louis asked.

"For a haircut."

Louis tucked his amulet carefully inside his shirt and patted the bulge it made there.

"Tell him to cut off just a little, O.K.?" he said.

"O.K." his mother answered.

Next morning Louis went downstairs in his pajamas.

"I don't feel good," he said.

"We're having waffles. Too bad. Go back to bed and I'll bring you up some milk toast," his mother said.

Louis got dressed so fast he put his sweater on inside out. He ate three waffles and could've polished off a few more. His baby sister sat in her high chair industriously stuffing her slipper full of oatmeal, as a cook would stuff a Thanksgiving turkey.

"How do you stand her?" Louis said to his mother.

"Nononono," his sister said, stuffing away like mad.

"Next time, somebody better teach that kid to say 'Yes,'" Louis said.

Miss Carmichael was pleased when Louis handed in his picture of a giant genie coming out of a tiny bottle as his contribution to the paper.

"Very nice, Louis," she said. "This shows a great deal of imagination." Calvin Leffert gave her a picture he'd made of an electric light fixture made of banana peels.

"Very interesting, Calvin," Miss Carmichael said. She never played favorites.

Amy Adams handed in a sheaf of poems.

"Amy dear," Miss Carmichael said, "I think we have enough poetry at the moment. Why don't you take these home and if we need more, I'll call on you."

"Fake out," Louis said to Amy.

At lunch time, Matthew exchanged a package of Hostess Twinkies for a hard-boiled egg. John gave Louis two apple slices covered in cinnamon and sugar.

"You don't even have to give me anything for them," John said. There weren't too many people Louis knew who would do things like that.

"You going to play football today?" Matthew asked.

"I don't know," Louis answered. He'd been debating whether or not he'd go to the playground. Yesterday had been bad. On the other hand, the day before yesterday had been good. He decided to give it one more try.

"Hey, you, you with the big ears," a big guy said to Louis. "Want to play right guard? We're short a couple of guys. You got in the game a couple of days ago, right? Get over there next to Harry and remember, you have to cross the goal line and touch the ball on the ground for it to count as a touchdown."

Louis was astonished. The way he'd said "You with the big ears" didn't even bother him. It was the tone of voice, the way he said it, like "You with the red hair" or "You with the brown pants." Louis put on his helmet and ran out to the field.

"O.K., guys, time for the huddle." Louis got squashed. He didn't really know what was going on. All he knew was he'd never been so happy. He ran from one end of the field to the other.

"Time for one more play," the kid named Jim who everybody listened to, said. "Let's make it a good one."

Louis stood alert, at the ready. Jim called the signals.

"Hey, get it, Ears! That's the boy! Run it all the

way!" Louis heard a whole bunch of voices calling. He looked up just in time: *whoof!* The ball landed in his arms and he ran with it. His legs churned so hard his knees almost reached his chin. He crossed the goal line and fell on his face. He still had the ball. He hadn't dropped it. He hadn't been stopped. He had made a touchdown.

Jim scraped him off the ground.

."You all right, kid? Nothing broken?" Jim said.

Louis smiled. His chin had a big scrape on it. His nose started to bleed.

"Did I score?" he said.

"If we were keeping score, you would've scored," Jim said. "You're all right, Ears. In a couple of years, you'll be lots better. You're a gutsy little guy, Ears, and that's half the battle."

Jim and Harry and Steve and Louis walked off the field with their arms around one another. Louis was in the middle. He had to reach way up to touch their shoulders, so far up that his arms were stretched as far as they could stretch. It was uncomfortable, walking that way. But he made it. Louis could've walked that way for miles, if he'd had to.

All of a sudden I caught the ball and I ran and ran until I thought I'd burst and then I went over the goal line and I made a touchdown and they told me I was a gutsy kid."

Tom's eyes were wide.

"That means you're a hero," he said. "If you make a touchdown, you're a hero."

"Only if you make the winning touchdown," Louis said. "Then you're a hero."

"If you score a touchdown, you're a hero," Tom said stubbornly.

"Oh well," Louis said.

"If Tom wants to think you're a hero, better let him," Louis' mother said. "I think it's wonderful and I'm proud of you, Louis, but I'm worried about you playing with children so much bigger and stronger than you. You might get hurt."

She washed his face and put Mercurochrome on his chin.

Louis finished his snack. "I'm going to see Mrs. Beeble," he said. "I want to tell her what happened." He was quite sure his amulet had been partly responsible. Maybe not all but part. That and the bar bells.

"Take her an onion, will you?" his mother said. "I owe her one. And here's a jar of apricot jam I made. She's a good old soul. I worry about her living there alone."

"She's a superior poker player," Louis said. He didn't like hearing Mrs. Beeble described as an old soul.

His mother raised her eyebrows. "Is she? You're pretty young for poker."

"We only use candy mints for chips. Mostly she wins and she gets to eat all the pink ones."

"That's good," his mother said. "It'll keep our dentist's bills down."

Louis knocked on Mrs. Beeble's door. She answered almost immediately.

"I've missed you," she said. Louis was glad to see she had his ring on her little finger. "Come on in and we'll play a hand or two."

"I came to tell you what happened," Louis said, handing her the onion and the jam.

She looked at his bruised chin. "You fell down the stairs or something?"

"No," Louis said, "I played football with the sixth graders and I made a touchdown," Louis said. "That never happened before. They said I was gutsy."

Mrs. Beeble shuffled the cards.

"I shouldn't be surprised," she said.

"And Jim called me Ears and I didn't even care. He said it like he was calling me a nice name. He said it like it didn't matter how big my ears were. He said it like he liked me."

"How could he help it?" Mrs. Beeble dealt a hand. "I told you a man with good-sized ears is a man with character. You've got character, Louis. That's extremely important and extremely rare."

Louis dipped down inside his shirt front and brought up his charm. "I think this really is a good luck charm, like you said. It brought me good luck. It and the bar bells. I lift them every morning and every night. My muscles don't look any bigger," he pulled up his sleeve for her to see, "but they *feel* bigger."

"That's what counts," Mrs. Beeble said, inspecting his arm.

Louis picked up his cards and arranged them in a nice little fan. "I bid one white," he said.

"I'll raise you two," she said, leaning toward him.

Louis held his cards against his chest.

"I'm just getting comfortable," she said. "I'm not peeking."

"I didn't say you were," he said.

Louis won the next two hands. Mrs. Beeble got up and turned around three times. "That's to change my luck," she said. "How about taking your charm off and giving me a chance?"

"I don't know," Louis said slowly, "I don't really think I want to."

"I was only kidding." She won the next two hands. "See?" she chortled. "Three turns in the direction of the west wind does it every time."

"I think you make some of those things up," Louis said.

"Sometimes I do but not always."

"Did you have a nice time when your niece and her husband came over?" Louis asked politely.

"They ate me out of house and home," Mrs. Beeble announced with satisfaction. "If my niece opens a can of soup, she thinks she's Betty Crocker. And does he ever like to eat! My lands! They took after my steak and kidney pie and didn't speak a word until the dish was empty. It did my heart good to see them. They want me to come and live with them," she said.

"All the time, you mean?" Louis said.

"All the time," she answered. "But I know what'd happen. I'd be chief cook and bottle washer and that I don't aim to be. Mr. Beeble never lifted a hand around the house but he was a hardworking man and entitled to his creature comforts. But my waiting-on days are over. I like living here by myself, doing what I want to do when I want to do it. I told 'em no in the nicest possible way. They say I'm too old to be living alone and to that I say 'Phooey!' "

"You know what?" Louis said, "I think you're gutsy too, Mrs. Beeble."

"Well, thank you, Louis," she said. "It's a good way to be."

When Louis left Mrs. Beeble's, he headed for the old man's house. He wanted to tell him about his touchdown.

He knocked on the front door. There was no answer. He went around back and when there was no answer there, he pressed his nose against the glass. He pulled back fast. A large white thing lay on the floor. For one horrible moment Louis thought it might be Agnes stretched out, her eyes on the ceiling. Then he realized it was a table or a couch, covered with a cloth to keep the dust out. He ran around to the front and looked in the window. Suppose Agnes was hiding inside, looking out the window right smack in his face? Louis shuddered at the idea.

"If you're looking for them, they're gone," a woman leaned over the fence and told him. "Pulled out yesterday in a U-Haul-It."

"Where'd they go?" Louis said.

"Who knows?" the woman shrugged. "Maybe Florida, maybe California. Some place warm, I shouldn't wonder. She was always complaining about her arthritis. If anyone asked me, I'd tell 'em I thought the bill collectors were after 'em." She sniffed and pulled her sweater close. "A man would come calling every so often. Looked like a bill collector to me."

"What's a bill collector look like?" Louis asked.

"How would I know?" the woman said angrily and went inside her house, slamming the door.

I have this neat idea," Matthew said. "You guys come over on Saturday and we'll try it out. It's really cool but I need help."

"What is it?" Louis said.

"My mother said she wants me out of the way all day Saturday," John said. "She's cleaning closets and waxing floors and all like that." He slipped a thick slice of cucumber doused in mayonnaise out from between two slices of bread and ate it. "I expect I could be at your house by seven or eight if I can get my father to bring me," he said.

"That's too early," Matthew said.

"You want to trade?" Louis said.

"What for what?"

"I've got cheese and relish."

"No," Matthew said firmly, "I've got cream cheese and walnut. I'm sorry, Louis, but I don't want to trade today."

"I don't know how you eat that junk," Louis said.

"I don't know how you eat the junk you eat," Matthew replied.

"Hey Dumbo, how's old Elephant Ears today?" It was skinny Ernie, sliding his way down the bench to sit opposite them. "I think your ears got bigger since I saw you last." He poked his friend with the tiny eyes.

"I think so too," the friend said.

"Anyway," Matthew went on as if he hadn't heard them, "you take a Havaheart and tie it to a tree or something so it won't float away, then you drop it in the river after you load it up with bait. Then, presto, a trout or pickerel swims inside and you've got him."

"You think it'd work?" Louis asked.

"It's worth a try," Matthew said.

"You're some sweet kid, Sugar Bowl," Ernie said, unwrapping a marshmallow fluff sandwich. "How'd you get so sweet?"

Louis flexed his muscles. Maybe now was the time. One good punch right in the middle of Ernie's

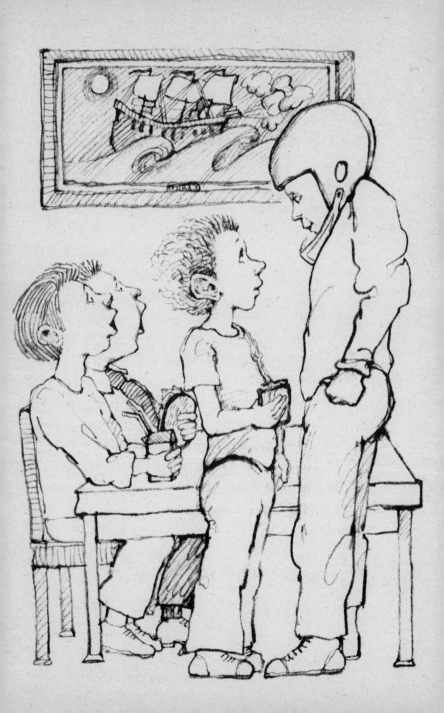

mouth. He'd really spray that marshmallow fluff around.

"Hey Ears!" It was Jim. "I'm looking for you. We need you, kid. A couple of guys are out sick and Steve said 'Go see if you can find that kid who made the run the day before yesterday. The little kid with the big ears.' So get a move on. You can finish your lunch on the way."

Louis got up, shoving the rest of his sandwich in his mouth. He looked at skinny Ernie who was sitting with his mouth wide open, the marshmallow fluff sort of drooling out. His friend with the tiny eyes was turning his head from left to right, like he didn't know whose side to be on.

Louis put on his helmet.

"I'm coming," he said.

"The big guys want me to play football with them," he said to John and Matthew. "I'll see you."

Then he turned to Ernie and his friend.

"So long, skinny Ernie and Pig Eyes. Don't take any wooden nickels."

Skinny Ernie closed his mouth and gulped.

"So long, Louis," he said.